I'M TRAPPED IN A
PROFESSIONAL WRESTLER'S BODY

TODD STRASSER

PINE HILL MIDDLE SCHOOL
LIBRARY

AN
APPLE
PAPERBACK

SCHOLASTIC INC.
New York Toronto London Auckland Sydney
Mexico City New Delhi Hong Kong

For
Princess Pam
Lanky Lia
General Geoff

No part of this publication may be reproduced in whole or in part, or stored in a retrieval system, or transmitted in any form or by any means, electronic, mechanical, photocopying, recording, or otherwise, without written permission of the publisher. For information regarding permission, write to Scholastic Inc., Attention: Permissions Department, 555 Broadway, New York, NY 10012.

ISBN 0-439-14773-5

12 11 10 9 8 7 6 5 4 3 2   0 1 2 3 4 5/0

Printed in the U.S.A.   40

First Scholastic printing, February 2000

1

"Neutron Neuman, The Human Bomb, throws a Russian leg sweep on No Nerve Nelson!" my friend Andy Kent shouted. "No Nerve comes back with a slingshot suplex into a frog splash choke slam! Looks like The Human Bomb has his hands full. No Nerve is eating him alive! It's an all-out war as these two titans of brawling beefcake rumble in the superfeud of the century!"

Inside the wrestling ring we'd built in my backyard, Alex Silver and I locked arms and tried moves on each other.

"The crowd here at the World Backyard Wrestling Federation is going nutzoid!" Andy raved. "The Human Bomb has all the moves, but No Nerve is a superstar in the making. This is pure mayhem. I promise you, one of these warriors won't live to see tomorrow, and the other will be a bloody and tattered mess!"

Andy was the announcer. Alex was Neutron Neuman, and I was No Nerve Nelson. We were

both wearing knee and elbow pads. We were trying to throw the other to the floor of the ring,
which was covered with old sleeping bags and
blankets. The corner posts were wooden garden
stakes. And the ropes were clothesline.

I stuck my leg behind Alex and tried to throw
him off balance.

"There it is!" Andy cried. "The jackknife power
bomb into the death drop! The Human Bomb is
going to try to come back with his patented
shooting star press, but No Nerve surprises him
with a flying chicken wing into a low-fat drum-
stick!"

Alex went down, but he pulled me with him.
We rolled around on the ground, trying to pin
each other, but mostly getting tangled in the
blankets and sleeping bags.

Then we heard someone clear her throat.
"Ahem!"

Alex and I looked up from the tangle of bed-
clothes. It was my mom, home early from work.
She was wearing her workclothes and carrying a
briefcase. Her forehead was wrinkled, and her
lips were pursed with concern.

"Do you have to do this?" she asked. "It looks
so violent, and I'm sure someone's going to get
hurt."

"Mom, kids have been wrestling forever," I argued.

"It's true, Mrs. Sherman," Andy added. "We

2

studied it in school. They even wrestled in ancient Rome and Greece. Like in Athens and Sporta."

"It's not Sporta," Alex snorted. "It's *Sparta*, you Jell-O brain."

"Sporta, Sparta, what's the difference?" Andy shrugged.

"Maybe they wrestled," Mom allowed, "but I'm sure it didn't *sound* so violent. I mean, power bombs and death drops sound awful."

"That's probably because the ancient Greeks didn't have bombs!" Andy said. "But I bet they had power knee catapults and slingshot discus crushers. Remember David and Goliath? You're talking the AGWWF!"

Alex made a face. "The what?"

"The Ancient Greek World Wrestling Federation!" Andy said. "Sam 'The Slam' Socrates. Pete 'The Potato' Plato!"

Mom gave Andy a strange look and then shook her head wearily.

"Just be careful, boys," she cautioned, and went inside.

As soon as she was gone, Andy spun around. "Okay, guys, it's my turn. Who wants to wrestle Brainiac?"

But before we could decide, our friend Josh Hopka rode up on his bike. "Oh, no," he groaned when he saw the ring we'd made. "It's the SWWA."

2

"What's the SWWA?" Alex asked.

"The Stupid World Wrestling Association," Josh said as he got off his bike.

"Get stuffed, Josh. We're having fun," Andy said. "If you don't like it, leave."

"I just don't get you guys," Josh shot back. "How can you fall for that junk when it's so fake?"

"That's not the point," I said. "It's entertainment."

"And it's not *all* fake," added Andy.

"I don't think *any* of it's fake," said Alex. "Didn't you hear that Stump Grinder Gershon put Leon 'The Hook' Fisher in the hospital for a month with a broken back?"

"Give me a break." Josh rolled his eyes in disbelief.

"It's true!" Alex insisted.

"Oh, really?" Josh chuckled. "I suppose you went to the hospital and saw him?"

"No," Alex admitted.

"See?" said Josh. "Leon 'The Hook' is probably on vacation, fishing somewhere."

"You're such a jerk, Josh," Andy grumbled. "Like you know it all."

"No, I don't know it all, but I know this much," Josh said. "That stuff you see on TV is one hundred and fifteen percent totally fake."

"It is not!" Alex insisted.

"Yes, it is!" Josh replied.

"You're such a mucous face!" Andy grumbled.

"You're a boneheaded, big-nosed mental basket case," Josh growled.

"You're so dumb you flunked recess!" Andy yelled.

"You're so stupid the mind reader gave you a discount!" Josh shouted.

"Your dandruff is so bad the principal had to call a snow day!"

"Your feet are so smelly your shoes hid in the closet and refused to come out!"

"Shut up!" I screamed.

"*You* shut up!" Josh yelled back.

"No, *you* shut up!" Andy shouted.

"*Everyone* shut up!" Alex bellowed.

Bang! The back door slammed and my sister Jessica stomped out of the house. Her face was red, her eyes were like slits, and her fists were clenched. She looked really mad.

5

3

My friends and I stopped arguing. Suddenly it was so quiet we could hear my neighbors' TV through their open window. Jessica stormed up to me.

"Would it be possible for you and your pea-brained friends to have just *one* conversation that didn't turn into a nuclear war?" she fumed.

My friends and I shared uncomfortable glances.

"I happen to have a huge test tomorrow," Jessica went on. "Since your stupid argument began, I've moved to three different rooms in our house to try to study, and you know what?"

We shook our heads.

"No matter where I go," my sister said, "I can still hear your loud, obnoxious voices."

"Maybe you should try the public library," Alex suggested.

Jessica's eyes blazed with anger. Her hands became claws, and she stepped toward Alex.

"And now, ladies and gentlemen," Andy started

nervously announcing, "the title match of the century, pitting the crowning champion of the universe, Neutron 'The Human Bomb' Neuman against the rampaging upstart Jessica 'Short-Fuse' Sherman in what promises to be the ultimate flesh-chilling, bone-crunching, stomach-churning, eyeball-rattling, nose-picking, finger-licking, down-and-dirty, monumental monster massacre of all time!"

Jessica stopped. A crooked smile appeared on her lips. "That was actually funny, Andy."

"Thank you," Andy replied.

My sister turned to the rest of us. "This is my last warning. If you bother me one more time with this stupid wrestling garbage I will personally break each of your necks. Understand?"

We nodded silently. With Jessica, you never quite know whether she is serious or not.

"And by the way," she said as she turned back to the house, "if you morons ever bothered to read the newspaper you'd know that one of those dumb wrestling shows is coming here to Jeffersonville next week."

4

Riiiiiiippppp! Pieces of newspaper went flying around our kitchen as my friends and I grabbed it all at once.

"Not the news section, dummy!" Andy cried as he pulled a page away. "It'll be in sports!"

Alex yanked at a section. "It's in entertainment!"

"It could be in business, you know," I said.

Riiiiiiippppp!

Andy held up both halves of a torn page. "Look what you did, dummy."

"Who cares?" Alex said. "That's just the news."

"You guys are seriously ill." Josh chuckled as he watched us.

"Sorry we're not as mature and cool as you, Josh," Andy said sarcastically.

"I found it!" Alex gasped, holding up a sliver of torn newsprint.

"What's it say?" Andy begged.

"Come on, read it," I urged him.

"Okay, okay." Alex scanned the story. "Wrestle-Insanity is coming to the Jeffersonville Civic Center. Tickets go on sale tomorrow. Oh, cool! Listen to this! There's going to be a limited number of tickets available for an amateur wrestling clinic before the main event!"

"Awesome!" Andy cried.

"When is it?" I asked.

"It's . . ." Alex scanned down the story. "It's . . . Oh, no!"

Alex let go of the newspaper and stumbled backward, then slumped into a kitchen chair and grabbed his chest as if he were having a heart attack!

5

"What's wrong?" I asked.

Alex didn't answer. He just stared blankly into space with his mouth hanging open and a stunned expression on his face.

"I'll get some water." Andy ran to the sink and got a glass.

"Is he okay?" Even Josh, who usually acted like he didn't care about anything, looked worried.

Andy handed me the glass of water, and I held it to Alex's lips.

"What is it, Alex?" I asked as he took a small sip.

"It's the worst," Alex whispered. "The totally worst thing that ever happened!"

"What?" Andy asked.

"I . . ." Alex took a long, slow, miserable breath. "I can't go."

The kitchen went dead silent.

Then Josh groaned. "I don't believe this."

"It's terrible," Andy agreed.

"No, you dimwit," Josh snapped, "that's not what I don't believe. I thought Alex saw something *really* bad. Like the obituary of his mother or something."

"I think he'd know if his mom croaked," I said.

"Besides," said Andy, "this is *worse*!"

"You guys are *beyond* stupid," Josh muttered.

"You sure you can't go?" I asked Alex.

Alex nodded sadly. "Positive. We're going to a big family reunion. My parents have been nagging me about it for months."

"Sorry, dude." Andy patted Alex on the shoulder.

"Yeah," Josh smirked. "I hope you can live through it. I mean, just think how horrible it's gonna be! You're gonna miss a bunch of fat, sweaty guys grunting and groaning and rolling around on each other like overweight walruses."

Alex was so bummed about not being able to go to the WrestleInsanity show that he actually decided to go home. Josh hung around with Andy and me and ate an ice cream sandwich. But then he got bored of us talking about wrestling, so he went home, too.

As soon as Josh left, Andy turned to me with a funny glint in his eye. "Guess what, Jake?"

"What?"

"I didn't want to say anything in front of the other guys, but you know my neighbor, Mr. Daly?"

"Yeah?"

"Well, I guess I never told you this, but he's in charge of ticket sales at the Civic Center."

I felt my jaw drop. "For real?"

Andy nodded. "He gets us tickets for shows and stuff."

"You think he could get us into WrestleInsanity?" I asked.

"I don't know," Andy said. "But you better believe I'm gonna find out."

6

That night around eight o'clock the phone rang. Usually I was in no rush to answer it, since it was almost always one of Jessica's friends. But that night I raced into the kitchen.

"Hey!" my sister cried as I grabbed the phone out of her hands.

"Hello?" I answered while Jessica gave me one of her best "what's wrong with you?" looks.

"Jake, it's Andy."

"Yes?" I said eagerly.

"Bad news," Andy said.

"You couldn't get us into the amateur wrestling clinic?" I guessed miserably.

"Worse," Andy said glumly.

"Worse? You couldn't even get us tickets?"

"Worse," said Andy.

"How could anything be worse than that?"

"No free hot dogs," Andy said.

"Huh?"

"No . . . free . . . hot dogs," he repeated.

13

"I don't get it," I said.

"What I'm trying to say is, I got four special backstage passes that allow us to go into the wrestlers' dressing rooms," Andy explained. "I got four tickets to the amateur wrestling clinic. I got four ringside seats. But Mr. Daly said we'll have to pay for our own hot dogs."

I felt a big grin grow on my face. "I think I'm okay with that."

"Yeah," Andy said over the phone. "I had a feeling you might be."

We were going to WrestleInsanity!

"You know, this is gonna be about the coolest thing we've ever done," I said. "I mean, cooler than switching bodies with the President of the United States. Even cooler than switching bodies with a movie star!"

"Funny you should mention that," Andy said.

"Why?" I asked.

"Well, when you think about it, wouldn't this be the totally most perfect time ever to switch?"

"No way," I said.

"Aw, come on, Jake!" Andy pleaded.

"Forget about it." I was firm. "It's not going to happen. After we switched bodies with the lunch ladies, I *swore* I'd never do it again. And I meant it! Besides, the Mini-DITS is toast thanks to some jerk bomb who tried to wire it to the lunch line rail."

"You don't have to rub it in," Andy muttered.

"I'm just saying, *what if* someone fixed up the Mini-DITS?"

"It's hopeless, Andy," I said. "The thing was wrecked. I'm sure Mr. Dirksen threw it away. Let's just go to the Civic Center and have fun. We don't need the DITS."

"Okay," Andy seemed to agree, "I guess you're right."

7

The next day at school, everyone was talking about the WrestleInsanity show.

"Special backstage passes?" Alex moaned miserably when Andy told him our plans. The three of us were walking down the hall to the cafetorium for lunch.

"Shush!" Andy put his fingers to lips. "Not so loud. I don't want anyone to hear or they'll get jealous."

"*They'll* get jealous?" Alex grumbled. "What about me?"

Up ahead we saw Josh waiting for us by his locker.

"Okay, guys, watch this," Andy whispered with a smile. He went up to Josh. "Guess what? We got our wrestling tickets."

"So?" Josh asked.

"They're better than we thought," Andy said.

"What do you mean, better?" Josh asked.

16

"Oh, you wouldn't care," Andy said. "I mean, you know it's all fake."

"Darn right," Josh said.

We walked a little farther. No one said a word. Josh scowled and glanced at Andy.

"I'm just curious as to what you mean by better," he said. "Better than what?"

"Oh, just better than your typical ringside seats," Andy answered casually.

Josh frowned. "How could anything be better than ringside seats? They're the best there is."

"Not really."

"You are so lame, Andy," Josh snapped. "The Civic Center doesn't have sky boxes. To get any closer to the wrestlers you'd have to be inside the ring."

"Or inside their dressing rooms," Andy replied with a smile.

"Inside their . . ." Josh's eyebrows rose. "You got *backstage passes*?"

"Shush!" Andy put his finger to his lips. "I don't want everyone to know."

"Wow, backstage passes," Josh muttered to himself.

"*And* ringside seats." Andy rubbed it in. "*And* we're going to the amateur wrestling clinic. But like I said, you don't care about any of that."

"Er . . . right," Josh said. "There's just, er, one thing. If you can get into the dressing rooms, you'll be able to get autographs."

17

"Oh, sure." Andy nodded. "Tons of 'em."

"Well, then I probably should go," Josh said.

"Why?" I asked, surprised.

"Because of my sister," said Josh. "She's a total wrestling nut. She'd go whacko if I got her some autographs."

Andy grinned devilishly. "Then maybe we should invite *her*."

Josh smiled right back. "Hey, sure! If you want that creepy little single digit female tagging along, be my guest."

"What's a single digit?" Alex asked.

"Means she's less than ten," I explained.

Meanwhile, Andy stopped grinning. "Maybe I don't want *either* of you to go."

We stepped into the cafetorium. It was already filled with kids. Some were coming out of the lunch line with trays. Others were hanging around the Vend-A-Lunch machines.

Amanda Gluck passed us carrying a lunch tray. Amanda wore superthick glasses and was our sworn mortal enemy because she always told on us when we were fooling around.

"Hey, Amanda," Josh said. "I hear Andy has an extra ringside seat and backstage pass to WrestleInsanity."

Amanda skidded to a stop. "Oh, Andy!" she gasped. "I'll do anything if you'll give me that ticket!"

8

Andy glared angrily at Josh.

"Guess you'll have to choose between Amanda or me," Josh said with a chuckle.

"Oh, Andy, please!" Amanda begged. "I swear, I'll do anything!"

"Would you give him your whole collection of Barbie dolls?" Alex asked. Amanda and her mom were Barbie doll collectors, and they were very, *very* serious about it.

"That's not fair!" Amanda whined. "That collection is worth a lot of money! My mom says it's going to help pay for me to go to college."

"How about giving him just one?" Alex suggested.

"Forget it." Andy made a face. "I don't want any Barbies."

"How about Facial Hair Barbie?" Alex asked.

"There's no such thing!" Amanda cried.

"Bad Breath Barbie," suggested Josh.

"That's disgusting!" Amanda wailed. By now

her eyes were starting to fill with tears. "You're just being mean. Forget it. I'll get my own ticket to WrestleInsanity."

Amanda stormed away. Josh rubbed his chin and looked around the lunchroom. "Gee, Andy, I wonder who else would be interested in your ringside seat and backstage pass. . . . I know! Barry Dunn!"

Barry Dunn was just about the biggest, strongest kid in the grade. He had short blond hair and wore a miniature skull earring. He was the class bully. And lately he'd been in a really bad mood. He was sitting a few tables away.

Josh started to wave at him. "Hey, Barry!"

"Stop!" Andy gasped. "Okay, Josh, you can *have* the stupid backstage pass and ticket. Just don't tell Barry, okay?"

"I hate to say this, guys," Alex said. "But it's too late."

Barry Dunn had heard Josh and was coming our way.

9

"Great, Josh," Andy grumbled under his breath. "Now look what you've gotten us into."

"Hey." Josh shrugged. "Guess you'll just have to deal with it."

Barry Dunn arrived. "You wanted something, Hopka?"

"Uh, actually, it was Andy who wanted something," Josh said.

Barry turned to Andy. "What's up, Kent?"

The last thing in the world Andy wanted to do was tell Barry about our ringside seats and backstage passes. We all knew that if Barry found out about them, he'd probably threaten to break Andy's skull if he didn't give him one.

"Uh, er, uh," Andy stammered as he tried to think of something to say. "So, uh, did you hear about WrestleInsanity coming to the Civic Center?"

Barry Dunn screwed up his face. "Are you stupid, Kent? *Everyone's* heard about it. I already got my seat."

"No kidding?" Josh said. "Which section?"

"Ringside," Barry said with a nasty grin. "Best seats in the house."

"Ringside?" Andy repeated with a look of dismay. I knew what he was thinking. None of us wanted to sit near Barry at WrestleInsanity. But now it looked like we wouldn't have a choice.

"Believe it, twerps," Barry said. "I'm gonna be right behind the safety rail. So close I'll be able to reach out and touch them."

The safety rail was a steel rail that went around the floor outside of the ring. Wrestlers were always getting thrown out of the ring. The safety rail was originally put up to keep fans far enough away so that the wrestlers would land on the floor and not on them. But wrestlers had taken a liking to the safety rail — they liked to smash their opponents' heads on it.

"So, you twerps going?" Barry asked.

We all nodded slowly.

Barry crossed his arms. "Who's your favorite wrestler, Kent?"

"Brainiac Bloom," Andy answered.

"Ha!" Barry laughed. "That little wimp who tries to outsmart everyone?"

"Makes perfect sense to me," said Josh.

"Why?" asked Barry.

"Andy admires the wrestler with the one thing he doesn't have," Josh explained. "A brain."

We all chuckled. Suddenly Barry turned to me and narrowed his eyes.

"What are *you* laughing at, Sherman?"

10

Of all the kids we knew, Barry liked to pick on me the most.

"Who's your favorite wrestler?" Barry asked me.

"No Nerve Nelson," I answered.

"Another wimp." Barry smirked. "Guess who my favorite is?"

"Uh, Demolition Douglas?" I guessed.

Barry shook his head.

"Mortal Mayhem Murphy?" guessed Alex.

"Nope."

"Rampage Rumson?" said Andy.

"Wrong again," said Barry.

"Barfbrain Benedict?" guessed Josh.

Barry shook his head. "Never heard of him."

"Scuzzball Skully!" said Alex.

"Fungusface Flanders!" said Andy.

"Bad Breath Barbie!" I cried.

My friends and I gave each other high fives. Meanwhile, Barry gave us a suspicious look.

"You guys making fun of me?" he growled.

"Oh, no, Barry," Andy reassured him. "We just got a little carried away."

Barry made a fist. "You're gonna get carried away, all right. On a stretcher."

Andy and I shared a nervous look.

"So, uh, who is your favorite wrestler, anyway?" Andy asked.

"Terry 'The Torturer' Tompkins," Barry said, and turned to me once again. "You know this one, Sherman?"

The next thing I knew, Barry clamped his hand down on the muscle between my neck and shoulder and started to squeeze.

"The vise," said Alex.

"The Torturer's favorite move," Andy added.

"Ow!" I yelped in agony, and tried to twist out of Barry's grasp, but he kept squeezing. The pain in my shoulder was really bad.

"Pretty awesome, huh, Sherman?" Barry snarled. It was weird how he liked to hurt people.

"If you say so." I grimaced. "Now, how about letting go."

"Why?" Barry pretended to act dumb. "Something hurting you, Sherman?"

"Very funny," I grunted from between clenched teeth.

Barry let go. I rubbed the spot he'd pinched on my shoulder. It felt really sore.

"See you wimps at WrestleInsanity." Barry

chuckled and strolled away. I was still rubbing my sore shoulder. Andy stepped close.

"Just think, Jake," he whispered in my ear, "if you switched bodies with No Nerve Nelson, what you could do to Barry."

Even though my shoulder was really killing me and I would have loved getting back at Barry, I shook my head. "No way, Andy. Every time we mess around with the DITS it means trouble."

11

I got on the lunch line. Josh and Andy had brought lunch from home that day and were going to supplement their meals with Vend-A-Snacks. As I stood on line, I had to admit that Andy's idea was really tempting. No Nerve Nelson was famous for being immune to pain. No matter how hard they chair-slammed him, no matter how many jackhammers and leg drops they handed him, he kept fighting. If I were in No Nerve's body and Barry tried the vise on me, I probably wouldn't have even felt it.

And then it would be *my* turn to get Barry.

I'd nail him with a roundhouse kick punch.

Then I'd hammer him with a flying head butt.

I'd blast him with a one-way ticket into the turnbuckle.

As he staggered around the ring in a daze, I'd whack him with a Russian leg sweep, deliver a dropkick or two, then climb to the top of the ropes and finish him off with a moonsault into an atomic death drop.

Yeah, I smiled to myself as I slid my tray down the lunch line rail. Forget about carrying him off on a stretcher. After I got finished with Barry, the only way he'd leave the ring would be in a body bag!

"Uh, Jake?" Someone yanked me out of my daydream.

I blinked and found myself facing June, the big, heavy, red-faced lunch lady Josh had switched bodies with the last time we'd fooled around with the Mini-DITS. I could still remember that heart-wrenching moment when June in Josh's body had achieved her lifelong dream of pole-vaulting. And then crashed to the ground and nearly broke Josh's neck.

"You look like you were about a million miles away," June said as she scooped some french fries onto a plate.

"I guess I was," I admitted. "So how's Poop-sie?"

Poopsie was June's cat.

"Oh, it's so nice of you to ask," June gushed happily. "She just had kittens. Papsie, Pipsie, Popsie, and Ralph."

"Ralph's a boy cat, huh?" I guessed.

"That's right," said June. "Burger and fries?"

"Are they boy cats, too?" I asked.

"No, Jake," June replied. "They're lunch."

"Oh, right. Uh, sure, thanks."

June gave me a plate, and I slid my tray down to the cash register. April, the skinny lunch lady Andy once switched with, was sitting there.

"Hi, Jake." She smiled.

"Hey, April." I handed her my money.

She leaned close as she gave me my change. "That *is* you, Jake, isn't it? There's not someone different inside, is there?"

"No way," I answered.

"Okay, just checking." She winked.

I picked up my tray and headed out into the lunchroom. I found Josh and Andy and sat down with them.

"The weirdest thing just happened," I said.

"What?" asked Andy.

"I just bought lunch, and April asked if I was really me. Like she was half expecting me to be someone else."

"Hey, what do you expect?" Josh said. "Is there anyone left in school you *haven't* switched bodies with? I mean, there's Mr. Dirksen, our science teacher. There's Principal Blanco. And the lunch ladies.

"And your dog, Lance," Andy added.

"He doesn't go to this school," I pointed out.

"He did when he was in your body," Andy argued.

"And so did your sister Jessica when she was in your body," said Josh.

"And you can't forget Mr. Braun," said Andy.

"Our gym teacher?" Josh gasped.

Andy nodded.

Josh turned to me. "You never told me about that."

"You guys are just proving my point," I said. "*Way* too many people know about the DITS."

"Won't do them any good," Josh said with a shrug. "It's all over now."

Just at that moment I glanced at Andy. He was smiling, but when he noticed me he quickly looked away.

That made me wonder. Was he up to something?

Or was it just my imagination?

12

"**A**nyway, we have another problem," Josh went on. "You think our parents will let us go to WrestleInsanity by ourselves?"

He was right. I shook my head. "No way. That scene can get way too crazy."

"Exactly," Josh said. "So that means someone's mother or father is going to have to take us."

Andy made an unhappy face. I knew exactly how he felt. The idea of one of our parents taking us to the wrestling match was a total drag.

"How could we have any fun?" Andy asked.

"It ruins it completely," Josh agreed.

"Maybe someone else could take us," I said. "Someone old enough to drive, but not, like, you know, really *old*."

"Jessica?" Andy guessed.

"Forget it," I said. "No way. She'd never go. And if she did, I wouldn't."

"Who else do we know?" Andy asked.

We searched our brains but couldn't think of

anyone. Suddenly the future looked dismal. We sat with our chins in our hands, feeling like a huge gloomy cloud was hanging directly over our lunch table.

And that's when Mr. Dirksen came by.

13

Mr. Dirksen was our science teacher and the inventor of the Dirksen Intelligence Transfer System, otherwise known as the DITS. He'd designed both the original DITS and the Mini-DITS to transfer knowledge from teachers to students electronically. But all they did was switch people's bodies instead.

Mr. Dirksen used to be my least favorite teacher, a mean, balding guy whose favorite color was brown. The kind of person you'd swear was already forty years old when he was born.

But then he and I had accidentally switched bodies, and he had a chance to look at life from a kid's point of view. And he'd married this really nice young teacher named Ms. Rogers.

I wouldn't say he became cool after that, but he definitely became nicer. He didn't always wear brown anymore, either. And lately he'd been rubbing some stuff into his scalp that was supposed to make hair grow. So far he'd grown some blond fuzz that you could only see up close.

"Hey, boys," he said.

None of us answered. We were all bummed about not having anyone to take us to WrestleInsanity.

"As the cowboy said to the horse, why the long face?" Mr. Dirksen joked.

"It's nothing you can help us with, Mr. D.," I said.

"Try me," he said. "You never know."

My friends and I shared a look. The only way Mr. Dirksen could have helped was if he was a wrestling fan. That was a joke. It was hopeless. But maybe it would be good for a laugh.

"You ever watch wrestling?" Josh asked.

"All the time," our science teacher answered.

"Good one, Mr. D." Andy smirked.

"I'm serious," Mr. Dirksen said. "You're looking at a major fan. Ever since I was a kid."

My friends and I frowned. It was hard to imagine that Mr. Dirksen was ever our age. And even harder to imagine that he actually liked wrestling.

"I used to live for Saturday night," Mr. Dirksen went on, with a faraway look in his eyes. "You should have seen those guys. Haystack Calhoon and Gorgeous George. And later on there was André the Giant and Hulk Hogan. . . ."

My friends and I scowled. Mr. Dirksen actually

sounded like he knew what he was talking about.

"You're serious?" I asked.

"Absolutely," our science teacher answered. "Matter of fact, I was there the night that Man Mountain Monahan put the death crush on Seymour the Snake."

"Hey, I read about that!" Andy exclaimed.

"Who's your all-time favorite wrestler, Mr. Dirksen?" Josh asked.

"Hmmmm." Mr. Dirksen scratched the fuzz on the top of his head. "That's a tough one. There have been so many. . . . But if I had to pick my all-time favorite . . . it would have to be No Neck Nelson."

"No Nerve's father!" I cried.

"That's right," Mr. Dirksen said. "No one was tougher or meaner than No Neck. And a dirty fighter? He was the dirtiest. Biting, eye gouging, there was nothing he wouldn't do."

The looks on my friends' faces went from disbelief to astonishment. There was no doubting it. Mr. Dirksen was a major wrestling fan!

14

"In fact," our science teacher went on, "I'll tell you something I haven't told anyone in years. When I was your age there was only one thing I wanted to be when I grew up."

"A wrestler?" Andy guessed.

"You got it," Mr. Dirksen said.

I had to grin. "No offense, Mr. D., but it's kind of hard to imagine you being a wrestler."

"The Mad Scientist," Josh quipped.

"Doctor Doom," suggested Andy.

"Professor Pocket Protector," I said.

"So you still haven't told me what you're all so glum about," Mr. Dirksen said.

"Andy got us these great tickets to WrestleInsanity," I explained. "The problem is, we know our parents are going to insist that an adult take us."

"And that'll ruin it for you?" Mr. Dirksen guessed.

"No offense, Mr. D.," said Josh. "But it's kind of

like getting this really big ice cream cone and you're just about to take a lick when the cone breaks and the whole thing slams to the ground."

"Hmmm." Mr. Dirksen crossed his arms pensively. "I can relate to that. But still, wouldn't it be better to have *some* adult take you than not to go at all?"

"*Some* adult might be okay," Andy allowed. "Just not one of our parents."

"Well, I can think of someone who'd do it," Mr. Dirksen said.

We all looked up. "Who?"

"Me," said our science teacher.

15

"But there's just one ticket," I said. "What about Ms. Rogers?"

"She's going out of town this weekend to visit her new niece," Mr. Dirksen said.

My friends and I shared a look.

"Uh, could you excuse us for a moment?" Andy asked.

"Certainly," Mr. Dirksen said. "I'll be outside checking on what kind of trouble Barry Dunn is getting into."

He left.

Andy leaned across the lunch table. "So what do you think?"

"Go to WrestleInsanity *with a teacher*?" Josh shook his head. "That rots."

"It beats going with one of our parents," I said.

"Not by much," grumbled Josh.

"Mr. D. isn't such a bad guy," I said. "I mean, he's been pretty cool considering how

38

many times we've gotten in trouble with the DITS."

"He's still a teacher," Josh argued.

"Maybe we could make a deal with him," Andy said.

"What kind of deal?" I asked.

16

A few minutes later, my friends and I finished our lunches and went outside. We found Mr. Dirksen lecturing Barry Dunn.

"So," Mr. Dirksen was saying to Barry, "have we reached an understanding?"

Barry nodded.

"Next time you'll go straight to Principal Blanco's office," our science teacher warned.

"Right," said Barry.

"Now I suggest you go back into the cafetorium and stay out of trouble until the bell rings," Mr. Dirksen said.

Barry trudged toward the lunchroom.

"What'd he do this time?" Andy asked as we watched him go.

"He was trying out wrestling moves on some unwilling victims," Mr. Dirksen answered.

"Yeah," Josh said. "He put the vise on Jake before."

Mr. Dirksen sighed. "Someday he's going to learn his lesson."

"I'd like to know when," said Andy. "Everyone in school is scared of him."

"Believe me, boys, his day will come," Mr. Dirksen said, then turned to us. "So how can I help you?"

"We want to make a deal," Josh said. "We think it would be okay for you to take us to WrestleInsanity under the following conditions. First, you can't hang out with us."

"But aren't the seats together?" Mr. Dirksen asked.

"Yes," said Andy, "but when we're sitting in them, you have to pretend you don't know us."

"As if I came to the wrestling match by myself?" Mr. Dirksen assumed.

"Exactly," said Josh.

"But won't your parents want me to keep an eye on you?" Mr. Dirksen asked.

"You can do that," Andy said. "You just can't act like you're with us."

"I understand," said Mr. Dirksen.

"Next," said Josh, "if the situation comes up where we have to talk to you, we don't want to have to call you Mr. Dirksen."

Mr. Dirksen frowned. "But you never call me that anymore. You always call me Mr. D."

"Even that's no good," Josh said.

"What would you call me instead?" Mr. Dirksen asked.

"Well, we might say 'Hey, you' or 'Yo, dude,' " Andy said.

"Okay," Mr. Dirksen said. "I guess I could live with that."

"And third," said Josh, "you know how at wrestling matches the fans get all crazy and excited and they yell and scream and jump around?"

"Yes."

"You have to agree that you won't do anything like that," Andy said.

"But if you're pretending you don't know me, what difference does it make?" Mr. Dirksen asked.

"Doesn't matter," Josh said. "You still can't do it."

"Because it would be embarrassing, right?" Mr. Dirksen guessed.

"Totally," said Andy.

Mr. Dirksen rubbed his chin thoughtfully. "I must say that you boys drive a hard bargain. But for the sake of seeing the show, I'll do it."

17

On Friday the only thing anyone could talk about at school was the wrestling show that night. Everyone was totally psyched. At lunch, Mr. Dirksen came by our table.

"I'll pick you boys up at Jake's house around five," he said.

"Hey, keep it down!" Andy whispered hoarsely while Josh glanced around to make sure none of the kids at the other tables had heard him.

"Oops! Sorry," Mr. Dirksen apologized. "I forgot I'm not supposed to know you."

He left.

Josh gave Andy a worried glance. "You sure about this?"

"It's too late now," Andy replied with a shrug.

"Ow!" Ollie Hawkins grunted in pain a few tables away where Barry Dunn had him in a headlock.

"Looks like Barry's pretty excited about tonight," I said.

"You know, we may still have a really big problem," Josh said. "Barry's sitting ringside. If he sees us anywhere near Mr. D., he's gonna know we asked him to take us."

"If we're lucky, Barry'll sit on the other side of the ring," Andy said.

"Uh-oh," Josh said in a low voice. "Look who's coming."

It was Amanda Gluck, and she had a smug smile on her face. That meant trouble. She stopped next to our table.

"Guess what, guys?" she said.

"Uh, you just discovered you have a new nose growing out of your forehead?" Andy guessed.

"No," said Amanda.

"You realized that your mother and father come from the planet Neptune?" guessed Josh.

"No," replied Amanda.

"You stared at the orange juice because it said, 'concentrate'?" I guessed.

"Wrong." Amanda stuck her nose in the air. "You know how you wouldn't give me that extra ringside seat? Well, I got one anyway. So there!"

My friends and I shared a dismal look. That was really bad news. Not only would Amanda *and* Barry be sitting near us, but one of them was bound to see that we were with Mr. Dirksen.

"That's great, Amanda," Josh grumbled unhappily. "Now why don't you go play with Monkey Brain Barbie and leave us alone."

44

Amanda immediately frowned. "There's no such thing as Monkey Brain Barbie."

"Yeah, you're right," said Andy. "He meant Belly Lint Barbie."

"That's disgusting!" Amanda replied.

"Not as disgusting as Body Odor Barbie," I said.

By now Amanda was in tears. "I hate you! And if Barbie were here, she'd hate you, too!"

Amanda ran away across the cafetorium.

"I can't believe she's gonna be at WrestleInsanity with us," Josh muttered miserably.

"Try not to think about it," said Andy.

18

That evening we arrived at the Civic Center with Mr. Dirksen. The parking lot was still pretty empty. We all got out of Mr. Dirksen's car and started toward the doors.

"Ahem!" Josh cleared his throat and jerked his head at our science teacher, who was walking with us.

Andy stopped. "Uh, Mr. D.?"

"Yes, Andy?"

"Remember our deal?" Andy asked.

Mr. Dirksen frowned. "But I'm not talking to you. Why would anyone suspect we were together?"

Josh waved his arms around. "Maybe because we're the only ones in the parking lot, and you're walking right next to us."

"But if we're the only ones, who's going to see?" Mr. Dirksen asked.

"No offense, Mr. D., but I think we need to establish a minimum distance from you to us," Andy said.

"Like fifty yards," said Josh.

"That's ridiculous," I argued. "He's gonna sit with us."

"But when he's not sitting with us, let's say he can't come closer than ten feet," Andy suggested.

Mr. Dirksen backed away ten feet. That made me feel kind of bad.

"I just want you to know that I personally think my friends are being jerks about this," I said. "If it was up to me, I wouldn't care if you were with us or not."

"Good thing it's not up to you," Josh grumbled under his breath.

"I appreciate that, Jake," Mr. Dirksen said from ten feet away. "But I also understand how Josh and Andy feel. And I really don't mind. I'm just glad you boys gave me the extra ticket."

Josh turned to me with a smug look on his face. "See? If Mr. D. doesn't mind a minimum distance between us and him, why should you?"

"Just forget it," I said.

We started to walk again. Pretty soon we got to the main entrance. A dozen ushers in green Civic Center uniforms were standing at turnstiles, waiting to take our tickets. I turned to Andy. "Got the tickets?"

Andy suddenly stopped. His jaw fell open and he turned white. "Oh, no!"

19

We stared at him in disbelief while he frantically searched his pockets.

"You forgot the tickets?" I asked.

"I don't believe it!" Josh cried. "No one could be *that* stupid!"

"Why do you care?" Andy asked with a sly grin. "I thought you were only coming so you could get your sister an autograph."

"Well, uh, that's right," Josh sputtered. "But to come all the way here and not have the tickets is — "

Before he could finish, Andy reached into his pocket and pulled out four plastic WrestleInsanity badges. Each one was bright yellow and had a metal clip so that we could attach it to our clothes.

"Here you go, guys," he said.

I had to grin. "Good one, Andy."

"Yeah, really funny, phlegm face," Josh grumbled.

With the badges clipped to our shirts, the Civic Center ticket takers waved us through the turnstiles.

"Gee, it's like we're VIPs or something," Andy said in awe.

We stepped into a corridor with green cinderblock walls lined with refreshment booths and souvenir sellers. The air smelled of hot dogs and nachos.

"Hey, check this out." Andy headed down the corridor. We followed him and came out in the main arena. Spread out before us were thousands of empty seats, all funneling down to the wrestling ring itself. At either end of the arena hung a giant white screen for replays and close-ups.

"Mad cool!" I yelled with a laugh as we started down the aisle that led to the ring. Here and there stood ushers who were supposed to make sure you sat in your proper seats, but as soon as they saw our plastic badges they'd smile and wave us on.

"Wow, it's like we *own* the place!" Josh yelled with glee as we headed for the ring.

We stopped at the steel safety rail and gazed up at the ring. It was lined with three levels of bright red ropes held up by black corner posts. The turnbuckles on the corner posts had bright red WrestleInsanity pads on them.

"Wouldn't it be cool to get into that ring?" Josh said dreamily.

"Just so you could prove it's all fake?" Andy teased.

"Drop dead," Josh grumbled.

"Hey," I said, looking around at the empty arena. "Where's Mr. D.?"

"Who cares?" Josh said with a shrug.

"Come on." Andy started up the wide runway that led from the ring to the doors where the wrestlers came out. The runway was lined with another steel safety rail. "Let's go backstage and meet the wrestlers!"

"Right!" I started to follow him, then realized that Josh wasn't with us. I stopped and looked back at him. "Aren't you coming?"

"Uh . . . I guess." Josh hesitated.

"You scared?" Andy asked.

Josh puffed out his chest. "Scared of those fakers? No way!"

20

A ndy led us up the runway and into a wide hall lined with lots of closed doors. A guard was standing in front of one of them.

"That's where we want to go," Andy said.

"How do you know?" I asked. "It doesn't say anything on the door."

"Look around and tell me what you see," Andy said.

I looked around. "I see a wide hallway with doors."

"How many doors?"

I counted. "Eleven."

"How many have a guard standing in front of them?" Andy asked.

"Just that one."

"Right," Andy said. "Now watch."

Andy walked up to the guard and showed him the yellow badge. The guard opened the door. Andy waved back at us and went in.

Josh and I looked at each other.

"How does he know about this stuff?" I asked.

"Simple," Josh answered. "Does Andy know much about school?"

"No."

"Does he know much about sports?"

"Uh, not really."

"About computer games?"

"No."

"Music?"

"Nope."

"Does he know much about *anything* cool or interesting?"

"I guess not," I said. "I mean, except wrestling."

"Exactly," Josh said with a nod. "Now, come on, let's go see what's behind that door."

21

Josh and I went up to the guard and showed him our badges. He opened the door. Inside was a narrower hallway lined with even more doors. As we walked along, we could hear voices and laughter coming from the rooms inside.

"These must be the dressing rooms," Josh whispered.

"You think wrestlers are inside?" I whispered back.

Josh nodded.

I stopped. "You want to knock on a door and see who's there?"

Josh bit his lip. Just then, a door down the hall opened. A huge guy came out wearing a tight black wrestling suit with a picture of a mushroom cloud on the front. His head was shaved, and his arms were as thick as tree trunks.

"It's Neutron Neuman!" Josh gasped.

"How do you know?" I whispered. "I thought you never watched wrestling."

"Well, uh, sometimes I walk through the room while my sister is watching," Josh explained.

Neutron Neuman headed down the hall away from us.

"Should we follow him?" Josh whispered.

"I don't know," I whispered back. "What if he's going to the bathroom?"

"You're right," Josh said. "He might not like it if we followed him. Think he'd try a broken sink drop?"

"Or maybe a wet toilet paper bomb," I said.

Josh winced.

"And don't forget the toilet seat head slam," I said.

"Okay, you've convinced me," Josh said. "Let's just see where he goes. If it's the bathroom, we'll go somewhere else."

Staying a safe distance behind, we followed Neutron Neuman down the hall, where he turned and went through an open doorway. Josh and I went to the doorway and looked in.

Inside was a big room lined with mirrors and tables. A crowd of people was hanging around. Some were wrestlers in costumes. Others were wearing normal street clothes. Andy was standing with a small crowd of people around a wrestler with wild brown hair and a thick mustache. I had a feeling it was Brainiac Bloom.

Here and there, people were sitting in chairs or

on couches. Some were watching a closed-circuit TV mounted high on the wall.

"Hey, look!" Josh nudged me with his elbow. Over in the corner Mr. Dirksen was sitting with a wrinkled old white-haired man. A four-legged metal walker stood in front of the old man's chair.

Josh and I joined them. Mr. Dirksen and the old man were having a lively conversation. The man talked and gestured with his gnarled hands. Mr. Dirksen smiled and nodded. When he saw us, he jumped up.

"Boys," he said, "I'd like you to meet my childhood hero, No Neck Nelson."

The old man grabbed his walker and started to pull himself up.

"Oh, that's okay," I said. "You don't have to get up."

"The heck I don't," Old No Neck replied. With trembling hands and shaking legs he stood up and leaned on his walker. Then he extended his bony hand to us. "Howdy, boys."

I shook his hand. Old No Neck Nelson might have been a shaky old geezer, but his grip was surprisingly strong and firm.

"Pleased to meet you," I said.

"Same here," said Old No Neck Nelson. "Any friend of Bill Burkson is a friend of mine."

"Ahem." Mr. Dirksen cleared his throat. "It's Phil Dirksen."

"Oh, sorry," Old No Neck Nelson apologized. "My ears ain't what they used to be."

"Neither is the rest of him," Josh whispered in my ear.

"Old No Neck was just telling me about the time he and Killer Kowalski took on the Four Horsemen," Mr. Dirksen said.

"Yup, that was one heck of a match," Old No Neck said. "The horsemen were flyin' all over the ring. And Killer, he was fit to be tied. So I grabbed one of them horsemen and I threw him into the others, and darned if they didn't go down like a row of dominoes. . . ."

As Old No Neck Nelson went on talking about the old days, I noticed that Josh was looking around at the other people in the room. All of a sudden I felt his elbow nudge me in the ribs.

"Look at that!" he hissed. "See? That *proves* it's all fake!"

22

Josh got up and marched across the room. Because of the crowd, I couldn't see where he was going. I turned back to Mr. Dirksen and his hero.

"Uh, it was nice to meet you, Mr. No Neck," I said as I got up. "Catch you later." Then I hurried across the room.

When I caught up to Josh, he had joined Andy. They were both in the crowd around Brainiac Bloom. Brainiac was talking and laughing with someone sitting in a chair, but I couldn't see who it was. I moved in closer and saw the top of a shaved head tattooed with a mushroom cloud. It was Neutron Neuman again.

"Remember the time Stump Grinder got stuck in a bathroom before his match?" Neutron was saying.

"Oh, right," laughed Brainiac. "He couldn't get out! They had to delay the match on account of plumbing!"

Everyone around them laughed loudly.

I caught Andy's eye. He looked puzzled. He leaned toward me and whispered something, but I couldn't hear it because of all the laughter.

"What did you say?" I asked.

"I said I thought Neutron and Brainiac were mortal enemies," Andy said more loudly.

Now Josh leaned toward us. His lips moved, but because of the laughter I couldn't hear what he said, either.

"What did you say?" I asked.

Josh said something about proving something, but I still, couldn't hear him.

"Talk louder," I said.

Josh rolled his eyes impatiently. He raised his voice and said, "This *proves* that wrestling is fake!"

The crowd went silent. I felt the hair on the back of my neck go up as I realized everyone was staring at us, *including* Brainiac and Neutron Neuman!

23

Neutron slowly rose up out of the chair. I couldn't believe how tall and wide he was and how thick his muscles were. His arms were two or three times as big as my thighs! As he straightened up, he blocked the light behind him and threw a shadow over my friends and me.

He stared down at Josh and narrowed his eyes. "So you think wrestling's fake, huh?"

Josh started to back away. "Well, uh, I'm not saying it's *totally* fake," he stammered.

"You're not, huh?" Neutron Neuman growled. His hands were the size of baseball gloves. He curled them into fists. The muscles in his arms and shoulders bulged and rippled with power.

He took another step toward Josh, and the muscles in his neck actually twitched! It seemed like he was really mad. I couldn't tell whether he was faking it or not. Josh kept backing away. His eyes darted left and right as if he was searching desperately for an escape route.

"Hey, chill out, Neutron." Brainiac came up behind and put his hand on Neutron's shoulder as if to stop him. "Leave him alone. He's just a kid."

"Stay out of this," Neutron grumbled and shook Brainiac's hand off his shoulder. "It's kids like this who are ruining our sport. We put our bodies and lives on the line every time we go into the ring, and then this snot-nose punk goes around telling everyone it's fake."

Josh was backing toward the door. Beads of sweat dotted his forehead, and he kept blinking his wide, frightened eyes.

Suddenly Neutron Neuman reached out with those huge hands as if to grab him.

"Ahhhhhh!" Josh screamed, ducked out of reach, and shot out of the room.

Behind him, Neutron Neuman broke into a big grin. Everyone relaxed. It was obvious he'd only been fooling.

Andy and I shared a look.

"Gee," Andy said, "I don't think I've ever seen Josh move that fast."

"Yeah." I nodded. "Isn't it amazing what being threatened by a three-hundred-pound maniac can do?"

24

We found Josh all the way down the hall, hiding behind the security guard who was checking people's IDs before letting them into the backstage area.

Our friend looked pale as he wiped the sweat off his forehead with the sleeve of his shirt. "Is he coming after me?"

"Neutron Neuman?" Andy asked.

"No, Peter Pan," Josh replied with a smirk. "Of course, I mean Neutron Neuman. That nut was gonna kill me!"

"Well, you really insulted him," I said.

"Yeah, saying he was a fake in front of everyone in the room." Andy shook his head. "What's wrong with you?"

"I still think it's fake," Josh insisted. "But I'll tell you one thing that's real. Those wrestlers are *real* crazy!"

"*Attention!*" A loudspeaker in the hallway crackled. "*All kids who have tickets for the wres-*

tling clinic should go to the warm-up room right now!"

"That's us!" Andy said excitedly.

"Know where the warm-up room is?" I asked the guard.

"Two doors down on your left." The guard pointed down the hall. A couple of kids were already going in.

"Come on, guys!" Andy cried. "Let's go! Now we're gonna learn the moves!"

25

The warm-up room was covered with wrestling mats. An older guy with thinning hair and stubble on his chin welcomed us. His nose was sort of flat and crooked, as if it had been broken half a dozen times, and he was wearing a gray WrestleInsanity sweatshirt. He said his name was Tony.

"Okay, boys and girls," he said in a raspy voice after about twenty kids had collected in the room. "Today we're gonna learn a little bit about professional wrestling. And the first thing we're gonna learn is how to fall."

The next thing we knew, Tony kicked his feet out and fell down on his butt. All the kids in the room giggled.

"Yeah, you may think it's funny," said Tony as he got back to his feet. "But you can't do nothin' in this business if you don't know how to fall."

"What if you don't want to fall?" Josh asked. "You just want to make the other guy fall."

"Everybody falls," Tony replied. "And what you want to do is fall on your butt, because that's where you've got the most padding. Now I want everyone to try it."

For the next thirty minutes Tony taught us how to fall backward and sideways and forward. He taught us how to break a fall with our hands and roll through a fall.

And it wasn't easy.

"What was that?" he asked me at one point after I fell on my butt.

"A fall," I answered.

"Listen, kid," Tony said. "You gotta make that fall dramatic, understand? You gotta *sell* that fall to the crowd. You didn't just fall because you decided to sit down. You fell because some monster the size of King Kong clubbed you across the neck with his forearm. You gotta *make* the audience believe it."

Josh smiled and nodded knowingly at Andy, who raised his hand. "Excuse me, Mr. Tony, sir, but are you saying we're supposed to *fake* it?"

"I'm saying you gotta get the crowd excited and keep 'em excited," Tony replied. "They don't want to see some guy sit on his butt in the middle of the ring. They want to see bodies flying all over the place. You want to be a good wrestler, you gotta be an acrobat! You gotta fly all over the ring. You gotta use every inch of it inside and out. You gotta entertain."

Next, Tony showed us how to pull a punch and at the same time stomp our feet hard on the mat to make a loud noise so it sounded like the punch landed.

"The crowd loves the noise," he explained. "You may miss with that punch and not even touch your guy, but when the crowd hears that boom of your foot against the mat it sounds like you just *creamed* him."

"So once again you're telling us to fake it," Josh assumed.

Tony put his hands on his hips and glared at Josh. "Listen, petunia, this ain't about fakin' it or not fakin' it. I've been in this business forty years. You want to know how many broken legs, broken arms, broken fingers, noses, and jaws I've seen? Hundreds! You go in that ring to put on a show, to give the audience what it wants. I don't know a single wrestler who ain't got hurt doin' that. And I even know a couple who've died."

"Yeah, but — " Josh began.

"Ain't no buts about it, petunia," Tony growled. "If you get hurt in the ring you either keep wrestling or go to the hospital."

Next, Tony showed us some simple moves, like how to do leg drops and knee drops and elbow drops while slamming the mat and making it sound like you're hitting your opponent hard.

"It takes two people to make these moves work," Tony explained. "The guy who does the leg drop has it easy. It's the guy lying there on the mat who's got to make it look real. He's got to flinch and grimace and let his head roll around like he's just gotten the stuffing bashed out of him. Remember, you gotta *sell* the other guy's moves to the crowd."

"Why don't you just make the move real?" Josh asked.

Tony gave him an impatient look. "Listen, petunia, imagine you're in the ring and you're surrounded by fans. They want to see a good, hard, knock-down-drag-out fight. They want to see it seesaw back and forth. One minute you're pounding your opponent's head in. The next minute he's pounding yours. Got it?"

Josh nodded.

"Now just suppose that instead of that, your opponent walks up to you and gives you one to the kisser so hard you're spitting teeth," Tony said. "You really think you're gonna stick around and put on a show for the next fifteen minutes?"

"Well, it's a fight, right?" Josh asked.

"Sure, petunia," Tony scoffed. "So tonight you get your teeth knocked out and tomorrow night you get a couple of broken ribs. You gonna be ready to wrestle the night after that?"

"Probably not . . ." Josh admitted.

"Wait a minute, petunia," Tony went on. "You're on the card for the next night. The promoters have been advertising your match for months. People have paid good money for their tickets 'cause they want to see you wrestle. Maybe you're the star, petunia, the headliner. Maybe you're the one they all came to see. Know what happens if you don't show up?"

"They're gonna be mad?" Josh guessed.

"Oh, yeah." Tony gave us an exaggerated nod. "*Real* mad. So mad they're not gonna buy tickets to see you next time, because you might not show up. And you know what that means?"

Josh shook his head.

"It means you're finished, petunia," Tony said. "You're not wrestling anymore. You're riding behind a garbage truck heaving trash cans and swattin' flies. You look at the greats. Gorgeous George, André the Giant, Hulk Hogan. They lasted a long time because they showed up when they were supposed to and put on a show."

"But you said you've seen hundreds of broken legs and arms," Josh reminded him.

"Right," said Tony. "And just about every one of 'em was an accident. But the promoters and the fans don't like it. You have enough accidents and miss enough matches, and you're out of business."

Tony finished the clinic by teaching us "ring psychology."

"You gotta work the crowd," he said. "You give 'em something to scream about in the beginning. Nothin' real spectacular, but a few good, solid moves. Maybe a couple of reverse slams, something like that. But then you gotta let them calm down and rest their throats. If you make them shout and scream the whole match, by the end they'll have nothing left."

"How do you calm them down?" a kid asked.

"Give 'em something simple," Tony replied. "Maybe a headlock, an armlock, whatever. You give them a minute or two of that, and then you're off again. You throw your guy into the ropes. He comes back and gives you a tackle. Next, you go into the ropes. You come back, he gives you a forearm. You go down. He climbs up on the first rope to give you a slam. You roll out of the way. He hits the deck. You give him a good kick drop or two."

"And then you slow it down again?" I guessed.

"You got it, kiddo," said Tony.

"And then the next time you get them going, it's with even flashier moves!" Andy realized.

"Exactly," said Tony. "And you always save your best stuff for last. Your shooting star press. Your Death Valley driver. The end's when you're diving off the top rope. It's when you bring in your garbage cans and chairs. You gonna shoot some guy out of a cannon and into the fifteenth row, you do it at the end."

"But who wins?" Josh asked.

Tony glared at him with almost the same angry look Neutron Neuman had given him before. "If anyone was gonna ask that question, I knew it would be you, petunia."

"But I mean it," Josh insisted. "I'm not trying to be a wise guy."

"You *really* don't know who wins?" Tony asked. Josh shook his head.

26

"Okay, petunia, I'll tell ya the truth," said Tony. "I don't know who wins, okay?"

"But that's not fair," Josh protested.

Tony rolled his eyes. "Look, petunia, life ain't fair, okay? But if you want to be a wrestler and you work hard and you do what they tell you to do, you'll get your chance."

Tony turned to the rest of us. "There's just one last thing, kids. You gotta have a gimmick. All the great ones had a gimmick."

"You mean, like Brainiac?" Andy asked.

"Yeah, except just between you and me, big brains don't have a lot of appeal in this business," Tony said. "You're better off with something like Neutron Neuman, The Human Bomb. Something *explosive*!" He checked his watch. "Okay, kids, it's time for the clinic to end. Go out and enjoy the show."

My friends and I left the warm-up room.

"That was incredible!" Andy gasped when we

70

were out in the corridor. "I mean, I feel like I know enough to be a real wrestler. All I have to do is come up with a gimmick."

"I know," Josh said. "You could be the amazing Explosive Hollow Head. The wrestler *without* a brain, so they filled his head with dynamite."

"Gee, Josh, you're so funny I forgot to laugh," Andy grumbled. "I'm serious, jerkface. I could be a wrestler. I *know* I could. I just need the right gimmick."

"I hate to say this, Andy," I said, "but I think Josh is right about one thing. It's going to take more than a gimmick. I mean, you have to be big and buff. Most of these guys go two hundred fifty pounds or more. And they have muscles on top of muscles."

Andy winced a little when I said that. I think he knew deep down that no matter how much he wanted to be a wrestler, he'd have to do a lot of growing and pump a lot of iron first.

From down the corridor came the excited shouts of fans starting to enter the Civic Center for the show.

"Guess we better go get our seats," I said.

Andy hesitated and looked back along the corridor toward the room where we'd met Brainiac and Neutron Neuman.

"You guys go ahead," he said. "I'm just gonna use the bathroom."

"You want us to wait?" I asked.

"Naw, don't bother," Andy said. "I know where to find you."

"Okay," I said. "Catch you later."

Andy went looking for a bathroom, and Josh and I headed out into the arena. Fans were pouring into the Civic Center and taking their seats. Lots of them carried big cardboard signs with their favorite wrestlers' names or messages on them. We joined the crowd and headed down the aisle toward the ring. All around us people were talking about Neutron Neuman, Brainiac, No Nerve Nelson, Terry "The Torturer" Tompkins, and a wrestler named Typhoon Thomas.

Suddenly a loud, familiar voice behind us said, "I got a feeling this is going to be the Torturer's big night. He's gonna turn No Nerve into a jiggling pool of limp, liquid Jell-O."

Josh and I froze. We both knew that voice. It was Barry Dunn!

27

I grabbed Josh's shirt and tugged him into a row of seats.

"This isn't where we sit," Josh said.

"I know," I said. "I just want to wait here until we see where Barry sits. Then we'll know what to do."

Josh and I watched as Barry continued down the aisle and passed us. He was with some older guy I'd never seen before. I assumed it was his older brother or uncle or someone. The Civic Center was crowded enough that Barry didn't notice us. And besides, just about everyone had their eyes on the ring where the first match would soon take place.

"But how are we going to know if he's sitting near us?" Josh asked.

"Look down at the ringside seats," I said. "See the baldish guy sitting alone and eating the pink-and-blue cotton candy?"

"It's Mr. D.!" Josh gasped.

"Right," I said. "So we'll see where Barry sits and then we'll know."

Josh and I watched as Barry and the older guy went down to ringside and found their seats.

"We lucked out!" Josh cried. "He's on the other side of the ring from us!"

"Good," I said. "He'll probably never see us. Come on."

We started to inch our way out of the row. Things were looking good. Barry wouldn't see us. That meant he wouldn't get to tell the whole school that we'd asked Mr. Dirksen to take us to WrestleInsanity.

Josh and I got back to the aisle. We were just about to start down toward our seats when a voice said, "Oh, gee, look what the cat dragged in."

It was a girl's voice. Strangely, it sounded familiar, too. I turned around and came face-to-face with Amanda Gluck!

28

Amanda was there with her mother. We knew it was Amanda's mother because she looked just like Amanda. They both had those thick glasses and mousy faces. Not only that, but they were wearing matching gray Neutron Neuman sweatshirts with drawings of mushroom clouds.

"I thought you had ringside seats," Amanda said.

"We do," said Josh.

"Then what are you doing up in these seats?" she asked.

"Oh, uh, we just wanted to see what it was like up here," I said.

Amanda gave us a funny look. "Well, I'll see you ringside."

Josh and I watched as Amanda and her mom headed down toward the ring.

"How could she come here with her mother?" Josh wondered out loud.

"I guess she figures it doesn't matter," I said.

"Maybe it doesn't matter to her," Josh said, "but are you thinking what I'm thinking?"

"That if Amanda sees who we're sitting with we're dead?" I guessed.

Josh nodded. "Toast. She'll tell everyone at school. And she won't even care if we tell them she was with her mother."

"Keep your fingers crossed that she sits on the same side as Barry," I said.

We watched as Amanda and her mom made it down to the ringside seats. They stopped and looked at their tickets. Mrs. Gluck pointed in one direction. Amanda pointed in the other. They actually had to walk around the safety rail twice before they figured out where they were sitting.

Then they finally sat down.

Next to the baldish guy eating the pink-and-blue cotton candy . . .

"Oh, no!" Josh groaned. "We're dead!"

I nodded sadly. It was the worst thing imaginable. Amanda and her mom were sitting *right next to us*!

29

Just then the lights began to dim, and the WrestleInsanity theme song started to play. A huge roar rose up as the emcee stepped into the ring and began to welcome the crowd.

"Ladies and gentlemen!" The emcee's voice blared out through loudspeakers all over the area. *"Welcome to WrestleInsanity! The ultimate in madcap monster mayhem!"*

The lights went out, and the whole arena was cloaked in darkness. Suddenly the air was filled with the loud booms and flashing, sparkling explosions of fireworks!

"What do we do?" Josh yelled over the bursts of bright, shimmering lights.

"We have to go down there," I yelled back, pointing to our seats. "I know it's bad, but we came here to watch the show. Maybe if we're lucky, Amanda won't notice us."

"Are you serious?" Josh asked. "We're sitting *next* to her. Even with all these fireworks, she'd have to have the brain of a speed bump not to see us."

"Don't forget," I said, "we're talking about Amanda."

Josh took in a deep breath as if he were preparing himself for a very dangerous mission. "Okay, Jake, lead the way."

We headed down the aisle. Now that the fireworks were over, the lights went back on. Everyone was staring at the ring as the emcee announced the first match of the night: Neutron Neuman versus Brainiac Bloom.

The crowd exploded with a roar of approval! Everyone's eyes were glued to the ring. Josh and I got to the steel safety rail and inched our way past Mr. Dirksen toward our seats.

"Oh, hi, boys," our science teacher began to say. "I was wondering what happened to you. Isn't this the — "

Josh quickly brought his finger to his lips and shook his head.

"Oh, sorry," Mr. Dirksen said. "I keep forgetting I'm not supposed to know you."

There were three seats between Mr. Dirksen and Amanda. Josh and I glanced at each other. It was a tough decision. Did we take the two closest to Mr. Dirksen or to Amanda?

Finally we took the two next to Mr. Dirksen. No sooner did we sit down than Amanda looked across Andy's empty seat to me.

I gave her a weak smile and watched as her eyes went from me to Josh to Mr. Dirksen. Amanda's mouth fell open.

"You had *Mr. Dirksen* bring you?" she asked in disbelief. "Wait till I tell everyone at school!"

Just like that our great night out became a nightmare. But I didn't have time to think about it. The crowd began to roar even louder as Brainiac Bloom climbed into the ring.

Josh nudged me and pointed at the empty seat between me and Amanda. "Where's Andy?" he yelled in my ear.

I was about to yell back that I didn't know when Brainiac Bloom did the weirdest thing. He came right over to the ropes nearest Josh and me and winked.

"Did you see that?" Josh gasped. "He winked at me."

"I thought he winked at *me*," I said.

"Maybe he winked at both of us," Josh speculated. "But why?"

We had no time to wonder. Suddenly the crowd's roar grew even *louder*!

Neutron Neuman had just climbed into the ring.

30

All around us, people were on their feet, yelling and screaming and holding up signs. Even though he'd promised not to get excited, Mr. Dirksen was jumping up and down and shouting. Little bits of pink-and-blue cotton candy were stuck to his mustache and beard, and they fluttered as he screamed.

Amanda and her mom were both on their feet, screaming for Neutron Neuman. Amanda was yelling so hard that little bubbles of spit foam were flying from her mouth!

Josh and I gave each other amazed looks. Everyone was going crazy . . . and the match hadn't even begun!

Clang! The bell rang and Neutron Neuman came out of his corner with his huge arms outstretched and his teeth clenched. Sweat was already dripping down his forehead, and he had a crazed glint in his eye. He stomped into the center of the ring and waited for Brainiac to meet him.

Only Brainiac wasn't there.

He was still in his corner of the ring, with a really strange look on his face. He was biting his lip, and his eyes were bulging out.

But they weren't bulging out with some crazy, wild, murderous look. Instead, they looked terrified! Brainiac's eyes darted this way and that as if he was trying to figure out how to get away.

Gradually, the shouting and screaming from the audience began to die away. People stopped jumping up and down and shaking their fists.

In the center of the ring, Neutron Neuman gestured for Brainiac to come out and meet him.

But Brainiac shook his head and stayed in his corner.

"Whoa, ladies and gentlemen!" shouted the emcee. *"Looks like we've got a problem here. Is it possible Brainiac has run out of ideas? Can it be that his big brain is no match for Neutron's big bulk?"*

In the ring, Neutron Neuman frowned and gestured again for Brainiac to come out and fight.

But Brainiac just shook his head.

Boooooo! Hisssss! The crowd began to boo.

"Are you Brainiac or a chicken?" Amanda shouted.

Neutron Neuman kept gesturing for Brainiac to come out to the middle of the ring.

Brainiac kept shaking his head.

The boos and catcalls grew louder.

"You're not Brainiac! You're Scarediac!"

Finally Neutron Neuman put his hands on his hips and gave his head a disgusted shake. Then he started toward Brainiac's corner.

"Looks like Neutron has lost his patience," said the emcee. *"If Brainiac won't come out, he'll go get him!"*

The crowd started to cheer.

Looking totally terrified, Brainiac began to climb up on the ropes.

"I get it!" Josh shouted in my ear. "It's a trick! Brainiac is acting like he's chicken. But as soon as Neutron gets in range, he's gonna jump off the ropes and power-bomb him!"

The crowd must've agreed with Josh because they all started to shout warnings.

"Don't do it, Neutron!" Amanda shouted. "It's a trick!"

But Neutron kept going, and Brainiac kept climbing up the ropes.

Even the emcee got into the act. *"Careful, Neutron. You never know what Brainiac has in that massive brain of his!"*

"You see how fake this is?" Josh yelled at me. "Everyone knows Brainiac is going to trick Neutron. But Neutron's still going to walk right into the trap."

By now Neutron Neuman had reached Brainiac's corner, and Brainiac had climbed to the top rope.

Everyone waited for Brainiac to spin around and power-bomb Neutron.

Even Neutron looked like he expected it!

But instead of turning, Brainiac started to climb down the other side!

"*Hey, this is no trick!*" cried the emcee. "*Brainiac looks like he really is trying to get away!*"

The crowd started to boo again.

With an impatient scowl, Neutron reached over the ropes, grabbed Brainiac by his long, wild hair, and started to yank him back into the ring.

"*Looks like Brainiac isn't going to 'get away' with it, if you know what I mean!*" cried the emcee.

The crowd started to cheer.

Brainiac held on to the ropes. Neutron grabbed him around the waist and tried to pull him back into the ring.

The crowd started to go berserk! Once again the roar was deafening

Suddenly Brainiac's eyes met mine. We stared at each other for a second. He said something. Because of the roaring crowd, I couldn't hear him. But I could have sworn from the way his lips moved that he was saying, "*Help me, Jake!*"

31

At first I thought I'd imagined it. After all, why would Brainiac call to me? How would he even know my name?

But then I looked at the empty seat where Andy was supposed to be sitting.

Andy, whose absolute favorite wrestler was Brainiac . . .

Andy, who'd even said he thought switching bodies with a wrestler would be the coolest thing ever.

No way! I thought. The Mini-DITS was fried!

In the ring now, Neutron Neuman was chasing Brainiac around in circles.

"Oh, boy!" cried the emcee. *"Brainiac's in trouble now! He's on the run, and Neutron's going after him. And that's a small ring! Sorry, Brainiac! No place to run! No place to hide!"*

Boooo! The crowd was jeering and booing. They were throwing crumpled-up popcorn boxes and soda cups into the ring.

I stood up.

"Where are you going?" Josh asked.

"To find Andy . . . I hope."

I headed back up the aisle. Just before I left the arena I looked back down at the ring. Brainiac was holding on to the ropes. Neutron Neuman was pulling on his feet. The whole thing looked like a giant slingshot. If Neutron Neuman let go, Brainiac was going to be launched into the fifteenth row!

"Let him go! Let him go!" Chanted the crowd. But I knew they weren't asking for mercy. They wanted to see Brainiac get catapulted headfirst into oblivion.

I went out to the corridor where the refreshment booths and ice cream stands were. Down the hall the guard was standing in front of the door that led backstage. I hurried toward him, flashed my badge, and was let in.

The door closed behind me, and the roar of the crowd grew more distant. It was quieter back here now. I hurried down the hall past the dressing room doors. One of the doors was halfway open, and I happened to glance in.

I skidded to a stop, certain I was seeing things.

I backed up and took another look.

Nope, I wasn't seeing things. It was Andy. He was sitting in a chair with his back to me, staring up at a TV monitor mounted on the wall.

32

I knocked gently on the door. Andy looked into the dressing room mirror. When he saw my reflection, he frowned.

"Can I come in?" I asked.

"Who are you?" he asked.

Just as I suspected!

"You're Brainiac Bloom, right?" I said.

Brainiac in Andy's body nodded. "How'd you know?"

"Uh, just a feeling," I said. "He switched bodies with you."

Brainiac nodded Andy's head again and looked up at the TV. It was showing the match between Neutron Neuman and Andy in Brainiac's body. At that particular moment, Neutron Neuman was sitting on Brainiac's head.

"I can't believe I'm sitting here watching myself get slaughtered out there," Brainiac in Andy's body muttered.

"How'd he do it?" I asked.

"A couple of knee drops and a body slam," answered Brainiac in Andy's body.

"That's not what I meant," I said. "I meant, how did he switch bodies with you?"

Brainiac in Andy's body lifted something from his lap. It was the size and shape of the Mini-DITS, but it was wrapped in silver duct tape. *Andy must've gotten the Mini-DITS to work again!*

"I don't believe it," I gasped.

"Neither can I," said Brainiac. "I mean, am I really gonna be stuck in this wimpy little body forever?"

"Not necessarily," I replied.

Brainiac in Andy's body glanced up at the TV. Andy in Brainiac's body was lying face down on the mat. Neutron Neuman was sitting on him and twisting his ankle. Andy in Brainiac's body was squirming on the mat and clawing at the canvas.

"Gee," grunted Brainiac in Andy's body. "That looks like it hurts."

"Is Neutron allowed to do that?" I asked.

"He's not supposed to," answered Brainiac in Andy's body. "But he's gotta make the show look real, and if that's what he's gotta do, then he does it. I'm just glad *I'm* not feeling that pain right now."

On the TV screen, Neutron Neuman had stopped twisting Andy in Brainiac's ankle. Now he was twisting Brainiac's whole body into a pretzel.

"Ooh!" Brainiac in Andy's body winced. "That looks *really* bad."

"Aren't you worried about your reputation?" I asked. "I mean, if your fans see you getting clobbered like this, won't they drop you for someone else?"

Brainiac in Andy's body shrugged. "Probably."

"Doesn't that bother you?" I asked.

Brainiac shook Andy's head. "Not really. To tell you the truth, I'm kind of tired of this Brainiac gimmick. I thought it would be really big, but it turns out the only fans I get are wimpy kids short on brains *and* on muscles."

"Andy'll be disappointed," I said, pointing at the TV screen, "you're his favorite wrestler."

Brainiac nodded Andy's head. "Like I said, short on brains and on muscles."

On the TV screen now, Neutron Neuman was standing over Andy in Brainiac's body, grinding the heel of his boot into the small of Brainiac's back.

"Ouch!" Brainiac in Andy's body grimaced. "That looks bad."

"Aren't you worried about what Neutron Neuman's doing to your body?" I asked.

Brainiac in Andy's body frowned at me. "Why should I?"

"It looks like you're in a lot of pain," I said.

"Better him than me," said Brainiac in Andy's body.

It was becoming obvious that Brainiac wasn't interested in helping Andy. Meanwhile, it looked like Andy in Brainiac's body was in terrible pain.

And not fake pain.

Real pain!

If Brainiac in Andy's body wouldn't help my friend, I decided to find someone who would.

33

I left Brainiac's dressing room and went down to the big room where the wrestlers had been hanging around before the show. The room was almost empty now. The only wrestler there was No Nerve Nelson, who was watching the TV with his father, Old No Neck.

On the TV, Neutron Neuman had rolled Andy in Brainiac's body into a ball. The crowd was no longer booing. Now they were laughing!

"What the heck's gotten into Brainiac?" Old No Neck was asking.

"Don't know, Pop," No Nerve replied. "But he sure ain't acting like himself."

"Uh, maybe you should go help him," I suggested.

No Nerve Nelson turned and scowled at me. "It ain't no tag team match."

"I know, but it's obvious that Brainiac's in big trouble," I said. "I thought you and he were buddies."

"We are, kid," said No Nerve. "But I got my own match against the Torturer coming up. If I go out there now, I'll have nothing left later."

"There might not be anything left of Brainiac later," I pointed out.

No Nerve just shrugged. "Sorry, kid, what can I tell you? It ain't happening."

It was obvious that No Nerve wasn't going to help.

If he wouldn't do it, who would?

I could only think of one person.

I ran back down the hall to Brainiac's dressing room. Brainiac in Andy's body was still staring at the TV. The taped up Mini-DITS was on his dressing table.

I grabbed it. "Mind if I borrow this?"

Brainiac in Andy's body shrugged. "Be my guest."

A second later I was back in the big room with No Nerve Nelson and his father.

"Uh, excuse me, Mr. No Nerve," I said. "There's something on this I think you should hear."

"What is it?" No Nerve asked.

"Put this on and you'll see." I handed him one of the headsets.

No Nerve frowned. "These are the strangest looking headphones I ever saw."

"A new advance in technology," I quickly explained.

No Nerve slid on the headset. I slid on the second headset and pushed the button on the taped up Mini-DITS.

WHUMP!

34

When I opened my eyes, I was lying on the cold, hard floor. Old No Neck Nelson was leaning over his metal walker and looking down at me.

"No Nerve," he said. "You okay?"

"I'm No Nerve," a voice behind us said.

Old No Neck and I looked to our left, where someone in my body was sitting on the floor with a dazed look. I felt a shiver run down the body I was now in and goose bumps lined my arms. No matter how many times I'd switched bodies, it always freaked me out when I saw myself without looking in a mirror.

"What are you talking about?" Old No Neck sputtered. "You ain't my son. You're that annoying little kid."

"No, Dad," No Nerve in my body said. "I know you're gonna find this hard to believe. But I'm your son, and I don't know what I'm doing in this body."

Old No Neck turned back to me. "You tell him he's crazy, No Nerve. He ain't my son. You are."

"I don't know how to tell you this, Mr. No Neck, sir," I said in No Nerve's body as I got up. "But he's right. Your son is in that body, and I'm in your son's body."

"You're *both* out of your minds!" Old No Neck cried.

"Jake?" It was Mr. Dirksen, standing in the doorway. He looked back and forth between No Nerve in my body and me in No Nerve's body. "Which of you is Jake?"

"Uh, I am, Mr. D.," I answered in No Nerve's body.

"What in the world?" Old No Neck sputtered.

"I'm really sorry, Mr. D.," I said in No Nerve's body. "I know I promised I'd never use the DITS again, but Andy's in trouble."

"That's Andy out there in Brainiac's body?" Mr. Dirksen asked.

"Yes." I nodded No Nerve's head.

"Who's Andy?" asked Old No Neck. "And what's he doing in Brainiac's body?"

"You switched with No Nerve because you wanted to go out and help Andy?" Mr. Dirksen guessed.

"I want my body back," said No Nerve in my body.

Just then a huge roar erupted from the crowd in the Civic Center. Mr. Dirksen and I looked up at the TV. Neutron Neuman was holding Andy in pretzelized Brainiac's body over his head and was threatening to throw him clear out of the ring!

"Go, Jake!" Mr. Dirksen gasped. "Before someone gets hurt!"

35

Running into the arena in No Nerve Nelson's body had to be one of the coolest things I'd ever done. I could see myself on the huge TV screens in the corners.

"What's this?" cried the emcee. *"It looks like Brainiac's good buddy No Nerve Nelson is coming to his rescue!"*

The crowd went berserk, yelling and shouting and screaming.

As soon as Neutron Neuman saw me, he dropped Andy in Brainiac's body to the mat with a thud. He went back to his corner and waited while I climbed up through the ropes. The crowd was screaming. Out of the corner of my eye I noticed Amanda and her mother both shaking their fists furiously because I'd come to help the enemy of their hero, Neutron Neuman.

I helped Andy in Brainiac's body untwist himself and get to his feet.

"Looks like Brainiac has decided he needs

some help!" bellowed the emcee. *"He's called on his pal No Nerve Nelson! Now maybe the two of them are gonna take on Neutron Neuman!"*

"Two on one!" the crowd began to chant. *"Two on one!"*

"You okay?" I asked Andy in Brainiac's body as I helped him into the corner opposite Neutron Neuman.

"You don't understand," he gasped. "I'm not Brainiac. I'm just — "

"Andy Kent in his body," I said in No Nerve's body.

Andy in Brainiac's eyes went wide. "How'd you know?"

"Because I'm Jake," I said in No Nerve's body.

Andy in Brainiac looked stunned. "You switched, too? You came to save me?"

"Hey, what are friends for?" I said in No Nerve's body. "The only thing I don't understand is how come you're not fighting?"

"Are you serious?" Andy pointed Brainiac's trembling finger at Neutron Neuman. "Look at that guy! He's huge! And don't kid yourself, getting banged around inside this ring hurts!"

Meanwhile, the emcee was stoking the audience. *"Could be we've got a triple threat match now, folks!"* he bellowed. *"It'll be winner by pinfall or submission. That is, if they follow the rules. But I have to say that, so far, this has been one of the most unorthodox matches I've ever seen!"*

The crowd was screaming and shouting and going crazy. And the craziest of them all was Barry Dunn. He was leaning against the safety rail waving his fists. His face was red, and he was screaming, *"Kill 'em both, Neutron! You can crush both of those wimps!"*

Andy in Brainiac's body and I in No Nerve Nelson's body gave each other worried looks. Barry didn't know it, but he was probably right. Neutron could easily kill us both. Meanwhile, Neutron Neuman paced around in the far corner of the ring, snarling and snorting like some kind of wild beast.

Andy in Brainiac's body gave me a nervous look and whispered, "What do we do now?"

"We better wrestle," I whispered back.

"Uh-oh!" the emcee's voice blared over the loud speaker. *"Looks like Brainiac and No Nerve are coming up with some fiendish plan! If I were Neutron I'd be thinking about reinforcements!"*

"We can't wrestle that guy," Andy in Brainiac whispered to me. "He thinks we're professionals. He doesn't know we're just a couple of goofy kids."

"Don't forget what Tony taught us," I reminded him. "The most important thing is to keep the crowd entertained."

Just then a huge roar rose up out of the crowd. Everyone was looking up at the big screens.

Andy in Brainiac and I in No Nerve turned and

98

looked. On the screen we saw a huge, long-haired wrestler wearing a leather mask. He was stomping down the runway, shouting at the fans, and beating his chest.

"Oh, no!" Andy in Brainiac gasped. "It's Terry the Torturer!"

36

"*L*ooks *like we've got the makings of an all-out war!*" the emcee bellowed. "*Two tag teams of sworn mortal enemies in the ultimate no-holds-barred, anything-goes death match of the century! But will they wrestle by tag team rules? Or are we about to witness total four-way anarchy?*"

The crowd was going absolutely insane! Barry was jumping up and down, waving his fists, and screaming so hard spit was flying out of his mouth. Amanda and her mother were going crazy, too! Near them, Josh was looking around with a puzzled expression at the empty seats where Mr. Dirksen, Andy, and I should have been sitting.

Terry the Torturer climbed up onto the corner post and stood there with his arms outstretched, bellowing at the crowd. The roar of the fans was deafening! In No Nerve Nelson's body I swallowed nervously. The Torturer was huge! Looming over us with his arms outstretched, he looked like some giant angel of death.

"This is not good!" Andy in Brainiac's body whimpered. "I mean, this is seriously bad. We're gonna die!"

"No!" I whispered back urgently. "We're gonna fight them! We're gonna give the crowd a show!"

Just then the Torturer leaped off the corner post.

Boom! He landed on the mat so hard that the whole ring shook!

Suddenly I was having grave doubts about wrestling these guys.

Andy in Brainiac must have seen it in No Nerve's eyes. "Still want to give the audience a show?" he asked.

"Yeah," I said in No Nerve's body as I started to climb through the ropes. "Let's *show* them where the exit is!"

37

I never made it out of the ring. Neutron Neuman grabbed me in No Nerve's body and tied me up in the ropes while Terry the Torturer threw Andy in Brainiac's body around the ring! I winced as the Torturer hurled Andy in Brainiac into the ropes. As soon as Andy bounced back he got straight-armed with a clothesline to the neck.

Wham! Andy in Brainiac's body hit the canvas hard.

"I know they call him Brainiac," cried the emcee, *"but right now I'd say he's not exactly the sharpest knife in the drawer. In fact, Brainiac's looking mighty dull to me!"*

Now it was my turn to get bounced and body-slammed by Terry the Torturer. The whole thing was a dizzying blur as I got thrown and twisted and slammed.

At one point the Torturer tied me in No Nerve's body up in the ropes and started bouncing me up and down like a yo-yo!

"Come on, fight, you no-nerve wuss!" someone was screaming at me. "Act like a man, not a little wimp! You're worse than the kids I beat up at school!"

I opened my eyes and saw Barry leaning over the steel safety rail, screaming and yelling. And he wasn't alone. The crowd was starting to boo again.

"I must say that in all my years of announcing I have never seen such a one-sided match!" complained the emcee. *"It's as if Brainiac and No Nerve Nelson woke up this morning and discovered they were different people. They've completely lost their pride! They've totally lost the will to fight! I sure wish someone could explain to me what's going on."*

I would have been glad to explain. The only problem was that at the moment I was in the middle of a painful abdominal stretch thanks to Neutron Neuman. And across the mat, Andy in Brainiac's body was squirming to get out of a reverse chin lock from Terry the Torturer.

And that's when the crowd really started to go berserk!

"I don't believe it!" cried the emcee. *"I swear, this is the strangest thing I've ever seen in my whole life!"*

Neutron Neuman loosened his grip on me, and I was able to twist around and look at one of the giant TV screens.

And there I saw what the emcee was talking about.

Old No Neck Nelson was hobbling down the runway on his metal walker.

He was shaking his fist!

He tried to yell something, but then he doubled over and started to cough.

But there was no doubt about it. He was coming to fight!

38

"*Now I've seen everything!*" screamed the emcee. "*That old guy coming down the runway is No Neck Nelson, the father of No Nerve. That guy must be eighty years old if he's a day! He was a big-time wrestler back in the old days, but folks, we're talking the Stone Age. I'll tell you why he's coming. He can't stand watching his son be humiliated like this. He may not have much of a body left, but he's got his pride. Neutron Neuman and Terry the Torturer, watch out!*"

In the ring, Neutron Neuman and Terry the Torturer let go of Andy in Brainiac's body and me in No Nerve's body. They retreated to their corner and started to whisper as if they were trying to decide how to take the three of us on.

Andy in Brainiac's body and I in No Nerve's body dragged ourselves to our feet. No Nerve's body throbbed painfully. And from the way Andy in Brainiac's body was limping, I could tell he was hurting, too.

"This has got to be a joke," I muttered out of the corner of No Nerve's mouth to Andy in Brainiac.

"Joke or no joke, we can use all the help we can get," he answered. "In fact, maybe he'll take on those guys and let us leave."

"You'd leave that old guy in the ring by himself with those monsters?" I asked in disbelief.

Andy put Brainiac's hands in the small of his back and groaned. "Right now I'd leave my mother with those monsters."

By now, Old No Neck had made it down to ringside. He let go of his walker and reached up with his gnarled hands toward Andy in Brainiac and me. "Come on, boys, give me a lift."

Andy in Brainiac and I in No Nerve's body bent over the ropes. "Listen, Mr. No Neck," I said, "I really appreciate you wanting to help us, but I don't think you should come into the ring right now. You could get hurt."

"You think so?" said Old No Neck. "Well, let me tell you something, Jake. I've been waiting my whole life for this moment. And I'll be darned if I'll let a couple of broken bones stop me. Especially when they're not *my* bones anyway."

"Not *your* bones?" Andy in Brainiac repeated with a puzzled look.

"That's what I said," said Old No Neck.

"Oh, my gosh!" I gasped in No Nerve's body. "You're not Old No Neck! You're Mr. Dirksen!"

39

"**Y**ou're darn right I'm Mr. Dirksen," replied our teacher in Old No Neck's body as we helped him up into the ring. "Why should you boys get to have all the fun? After all, who invented the DITS in the first place?"

"You did, Mr. No Neck . . . er, I mean, Mr. D.," I said in No Nerve's body. "But don't you think the real Mr. No Neck is going to be kind of upset if you break all his bones?"

"You kids think old people are so feeble," said Mr. Dirksen in No Neck's body. "Just let me have that walker and I'll show you a thing or two."

"Uh-oh! Look out, folks! Here come the reinforcements!" cried the emcee. *"Old No Neck's brought his walker with him! Talk about a wrestler who needs a crutch! Next thing you know he'll be fighting in a wheelchair! This match is definitely one for the ages! The old ages! You younger kids are in for a real treat. You're gonna see moves you never saw before — mostly*

107

because they've been out of style for two hundred years!

Mr. Dirksen in Old No Neck's body hobbled out toward the center of the ring on his walker and gestured for the two monsters in the opposite corner to fight him. Neutron Neuman and Terry the Torturer glanced at each other and grinned.

"I sure hope they're gentle with that old guy," said the emcee. *"Otherwise, they might just as well put him in a full body cast and forget about him."*

Terry the Torturer started to climb up the ropes in the corner.

"Oh, brother!" cried the emcee. *"This looks bad. I think the Torturer means to take Old No Neck out of the match with one flying bomb! He's just gonna flatten the old geezer! You've heard of a flapjack? Well, you're about to see one flat Jack!"*

Terry the Torturer bounced up and down on the ropes like someone on the end of a diving board. Then he sprang way up into the air, did a flip, and headed down.

I closed No Nerve's eyes. I couldn't bear to watch. In a couple of seconds the only thing left of Old No Neck was going to be a couple of broken limbs scattered around the ring.

40

Wham! Terry the Torturer hit the mat so hard it shook. I opened my eyes, expecting to see little pieces of Old No Neck. Instead, Terry the Torturer was lying facedown on the mat!

Mr. Dirksen in Old No Neck's body must have rolled out of the way at the very last moment!

"Now, there's something you don't see every day!" the emcee shouted. *"The old guy moved, and the Torturer did a solo face plant! Ow, that has got to hurt!"*

"Grrrraaahhhhh!" Seeing his partner out cold on the mat, Neutron Neuman went berserk and charged.

Mr. Dirksen in Old No Neck's body slid the walker in Neutron's path.

Crash! Neutron smashed into the walker and toppled over it, landing facefirst on the mat next to Terry the Torturer.

"Come on, boys, let's finish them off!" Mr. Dirksen in Old No Neck's body waved to Andy in

Brainiac and me in No Nerve. Together we grabbed the Torturer and slid him out of the ring and onto the floor.

The crowd roared, but one voice rose above all the others.

"You guys stink!" Barry shouted from the other side of the steel safety rail. He was red-faced and spitting again. "You're wimps! You needed an old man to help you win! I could beat both of you with one hand tied behind my back!"

Andy in Brainiac's body and I in No Nerve's body gave each other a look. I had a feeling he was thinking the same thing I was. You weren't supposed to bring fans into a wrestling match.

Then again, you weren't supposed to switch bodies with wrestlers, either.

And it sure would be nice to teach Barry Dunn a lesson.

41

"**H**ey! Wait! Stop! Put me down! Help!" Barry screamed and pleaded as Andy in Brainiac's body and I in No Nerve's body lifted him over the steel safety rail and threw him into the ring.

"Talk about a scene that's gotten totally out of hand!" the emcee shouted. *"Now they're dragging fans into the ring! This could be the craziest match of all time!"*

Andy in Brainiac and I in No Nerve jumped into the ring. Barry stood in the middle of the ring, shaking and looking white as a sheet.

"Hey, guys, really, I was only kidding!" he gasped in a quavering voice. "I didn't mean it when I said I could beat both of you with one hand tied behind my back. Honest. I was just a little excited, that's all."

Andy in Brainiac's body gave me a wink. Then he turned to Barry. "I guess we misunderstood you."

"Yeah, exactly." Barry nodded eagerly. "It was just a big misunderstanding."

"Let's shake on it," said Andy in Brainiac. He held his hand out to Barry as if he wanted to shake.

Barry reached out and took Andy in Brainiac's hand.

A definite bad move!

"*Ahhhhhhhhh!*" The next thing Barry knew, Andy in Brainiac yanked him clear across the mat and threw him into the ropes. Barry bounced off the ropes and came flying back. This time I grabbed him and threw him into the ropes on the other side of the ring. *Boing!* Barry bounced back like a human pinball.

Andy held Brainiac's arm out stiffly.

Clunk! Barry hit it and went straight down on the mat.

Slap! Andy in Brainiac and I in No Nerve's body shared a high five.

Barry was on his back on the mat not far from where Neutron Neuman still laid facedown. His eyes appeared to be rolling around loosely in his head.

"*Boy, oh, boy!*" ranted the emcee. "*That's one fan who isn't just seeing stars. He's seeing whole galaxies!*"

"Good work, boys." Mr. Dirksen in Old No Neck's body shuffled over on his walker. "I couldn't have done a better job myself. Now, let's

112

get rid of Neutron Neuman, and we can consider this job done."

Neutron was still lying groggily on the mat. As Andy in Brainiac's body and I in No Nerve's body reached down to grab his arms, one loud, shrill voice reached our ears.

"I hate you! You really stink and you're cheaters! I bet you don't brush your teeth and have bad breath, too!"

It was Amanda, as red-faced and furious as I'd ever seen her. As Andy in Brainiac's body and I in No Nerve's body lifted the dazed Neutron Neuman to his feet, we gave each other curious looks.

"What do you think?" Andy asked.

I shook No Nerve's head. "I know it's tempting, but it's not like Barry. She may be a pest, but she's never picked on us or anything."

Andy nodded Brainiac's head. "Yeah, I guess you're right. Too bad."

"*Arrrrrrggggggghhhhhhhhh!*" The loud, furious roar caught us both by surprise. We spun around just in time to see Terry the Torturer come across the ring swinging a folding chair!

42

Andy and I managed to duck out of the way in the nick of time!

Clang! The folding chair hit Neutron Neuman square in the face.

The next thing we knew, Neutron Neuman flew out of the ring! Somehow he managed to land on his feet. He staggered backward and fell over the safety rail.

Right into Amanda!

Ring! Ring! Ring! The bell rang! The match was over!

"You'll never see a wrestling match like that again, folks!" the emcee shouted. *"And you probably wouldn't want to if you had the choice! But the winners are Brainiac, No Nerve Nelson, and his father, Old No Neck!"*

"Boooooo!" *"Hiissss!"* *"You guys stink!"* The crowd definitely didn't like the outcome of the match. We were pelted with empty soda cups and cotton candy sticks.

"Looks like it's time to go, boys," Mr. Dirksen in Old No Neck's body said. "Somebody better give me a ride."

Andy in Brainiac's body picked him up and put him on my back. In No Nerve's body I trotted back up the runway. Andy in Brainiac's body followed with Old No Neck's walker. The crowd continued to boo and scream at us. They shook their fists angrily and called us every name you could imagine.

I was really glad to get past the guard and go into the hall where the dressing rooms were. At least we were safe here.

Or so I thought until I heard someone shout, "There they are! Let's get 'em!"

43

It was the weirdest sight. If I hadn't known better, I would have thought I was watching Mr. Dirksen, Andy, and myself running toward us. Of course, it was really Brainiac, No Nerve, and his father, Old No Neck, in our bodies.

"We want our bodies back," shouted No Nerve in my body.

"Okay, okay," I said in his body. "We'll give 'em back."

"Right now!" demanded Old No Neck in Mr. Dirksen's body.

"Uh, just out of curiosity," I said to Old No Neck, "I can understand why these other guys want their bodies back. But you're so old and rickety. Why don't you want to stay in Mr. Dirksen's body?"

"Are you serious?" Old No Neck in Mr. Dirksen's body sputtered. "I just found out this guy's a science teacher!"

Brainiac in Andy's body held up the taped-over

Mini-DITS. "Look, I got the thing right here. Now let's do it, okay? I always wondered what it was like to be in a wimp's body, and now that I know, I want out."

"Okay, okay," Andy in Brainiac's body grumbled. "You don't have to get so personal about it, do you?"

No Nerve in my body pushed open a dressing room door. "Come on, we'll do it in here."

We all crowded into the dressing room.

"I'm going first," insisted Old No Neck in Mr. Dirksen's body. "I can't tell you how much I hate the idea of being a science teacher."

I started to hand out the headsets.

Just then the door flew open and someone shouted, "Stop!"

44

It was Josh. He was red-faced and breathing hard. It was obvious that he'd been running. Now he stared at all of us and wrinkled his forehead.

"Who's who?" he panted.

"Don't matter, kid," answered Old No Neck in Mr. Dirksen's body. "Because who's who now ain't who they're gonna be in a couple of minutes."

Josh ignored him and stared at me in No Nerve's body. "That you, Jake?"

I nodded No Nerve's head. "What's up?"

"You gotta give me a chance, too," Josh begged. "Come on, you guys can't have all the fun."

"Hey," said No Nerve in my body, "aren't you the kid who said it was all fake?"

"Yeah, but — " Josh gasped. "Oh, come on, guys! I deserve a shot, too."

Just then I felt someone nudge me. It was Andy in Brainiac's body. He jerked his head slightly toward the TV monitor in the dressing room. On the TV I could see Neutron Neuman and Terry the Torturer trudging slowly up the runway toward the doors that led backstage. Terry the Torturer was carrying a metal chair, and Neutron Neuman had what looked like a broken table leg. They both looked grim and determined.

Andy in Brainiac's body and I in No Nerve's body smiled at each other and turned to Josh.

"Okay, Josh," I said. "Which of us would you like to be?"

Josh looked back and forth between Andy in Brainiac's body and me in No Nerve's body.

"No offense, Andy, but I want to be No Nerve," Josh said.

"Hey, wait a minute!" No Nerve in my body argued as Josh and I slid on the Mini-DITS headsets. "That's *my* body!"

"Sorry," I said in his body. "We just need it for a few minutes more."

WHUMP! The Mini-DITS went off. The next thing I knew, I was in Josh's body and Josh was now in No Nerve's Body.

Brainiac in Andy's body yanked the headsets away. "No one's borrowing my body again." He slid one headset on himself in Andy's body and the other on Andy in his body.

WHUMP! A second later, Brainiac and Andy

were back in their old bodies again. Meanwhile, Josh in No Nerve's body was flexing the wrestler's big muscles.

"This is mad cool!" he grinned. "I'm like, indestructible!"

Crash! Behind us the door was smashed into splinters as if it had been hit with a battering ram!

Outside stood Terry the Torturer with his chair and Neutron Neuman with the table leg. Their eyes were slits of total fury and their jaws were clenched.

"What do you guys want?" Josh in No Nerve's body asked.

"Revenge," growled Terry the Torturer.

45

"Very funny, guys," Josh grumbled at school the next day. We were in the cafetorium, having lunch. "You guys are just a total laugh riot."

"Hey, you're the one who said you wanted to have some fun," I reminded him.

"Yeah, right," Josh muttered. "So you let me switch with No Nerve Nelson just as those two giant nutwads show up with their chairs and table legs."

Andy and I grinned at each other. It had been a great night and there'd been some cool battles, but the best of all was the one the crowd never saw because it happened backstage. The one where Terry the Torturer and Neutron Neuman went after Brainiac and the person they thought was No Nerve Nelson. Even the *real* No Nerve was glad to let Josh have his body when he saw how mad those two monsters were.

"Still think wrestling's fake?" Andy asked.

"Sometimes," Josh said. "But not when those guys get mad."

Josh should have known. We didn't get to switch him out of No Nerve's body until he'd been thrown out a window and had fallen two floors into a Dumpster filled with garbage.

Amanda came by with a lunch tray. She had a big bump on her forehead. Expecting her to say something nasty, my friends and I shared a nervous look.

But she walked right past us.

"Hey, Amanda?" I said.

She stopped and looked back at me. "What?"

"How'd you get that bump?" I asked.

"I don't really remember," she said. "Mom says it happened at WrestleInsanity last night. But I can't remember a thing."

"Serious?" Josh asked.

"Not a thing," Amanda said, and turned away.

"All right!" My friends and I shared a high five. But our celebration was cut short . . . by the arrival of Barry Dunn.

46

Barry had a couple of bumps on his forehead, too. One of his eyes looked puffy and black-and-blue, and his lower lip was swollen. He looked like he'd gotten pretty roughed up.

"You guys go to WrestleInsanity last night?" he asked.

My friends and I nodded slowly.

"You saw what happened to me?" he asked.

We nodded.

Barry wrinkled his bumpy forehead. The next thing we knew, he sat down with us at our table. My friends and I shared nervous glances. Barry had never done anything like this before. He leaned toward us.

"Have you told anyone?" he whispered.

My friends and I shook our heads.

"You sure?" Barry asked.

"Honest, Barry," I said. "We haven't told a soul."

Barry's eyes darted back and forth between us. "You *positive*?"

"Positive," said Andy.

Barry nodded and bit his swollen lip. "Okay, guys, what do I have to do to make sure you never, ever tell anyone what happened?"

"Uh . . . promise you'll never pick on us again?" Andy asked.

"It's a deal," said Barry.

"No, wait," I said. "Promise you'll never pick on *anyone* in this school again."

"Okay, you got it," promised Barry. "Word of honor." He held out his hand. "Shake on it?"

Remembering the night before, my friends and I hesitated.

"Hey, it's no trick," Barry assured us. "I mean it."

Slowly, one by one, each of us shook his hand.

"Okay," Barry said when we'd finished. "We've given our word. You won't tell, and I won't pick on anyone."

He turned and left the cafetorium.

For a moment, no one at our table spoke.

"Do you believe that?" Andy finally asked.

"I . . . I guess so," I said.

Josh grinned.

"What's so funny?" Andy asked.

"Know what I think?" Josh leaned back and put his hands behind his head. "I think I just became a *major* fan of pro wrestling!"